In the Great Meadow

Discard

To the memory of my father,
my forever storyteller.
S.C.

©1994 Skid Crease (text)
©1994 Jan Thornhill (art)
Designed by Brian Bean

Annick Press Ltd.

Annick Press gratefully acknowledges the support of the Canada Council and the Ontario Arts Council.

Canadian Cataloguing in Publication Data
Crease, Skid
In the great meadow

ISBN 1-55037-999-2 (bound) ISBN 1-55037-998-4 (pbk.)

I. Thornhill, Jan. II. Title.

PS8555.R33I6 1994   jC813'.54   C94-931163-4
PZ7.C73In 1994

Distributed in Canada by:
Firefly Books Ltd.
250 Sparks Ave.
Willowdale, ON M2H 2S4
Published in the U.S.A. by Annick Press (U.S.) Ltd.
Distributed in the U.S.A. by:
Firefly Books (U.S.) Inc.
P.O. Box 1338
Ellicott Station
Buffalo, NY 14205

Printed on acid-free paper.

Printed and bound in Canada by D.W. Friesen & Sons, Altona, Manitoba.

In the Great Meadow

written by Skid Crease

illustrated by Jan Thornhill

Annick Press Ltd.
Toronto • New York

The sun had just risen above the golden reeds of the pond when Frog-child hopped up to his mother and said, "Momma! I want to go exploring."

"Why don't you go down to the mud flats at the edge of the pond?" said Momma-frog.

"I went to the mud flats yesterday!"

"Then try the swamp-grass bog where the river flows into the pond," suggested Momma-frog.

"Momma, I explored the swamp-grass bog the day before yesterday! I want to cross the mud flats, hop past the swamp-grass bog and go out into the great meadow."

"The great meadow! Are you out of your mind?" shouted Momma-frog. "Why, there are things out there that will scratch and claw and eat you up! Don't you even think about going out into the great meadow!"

"Oh, Momma," sighed Frog-child, "I'm not a little tadpole anymore. It's time you let me grow up and go out exploring."

Momma-frog looked lovingly at Frog-child.
"I suppose you're right, but it's hard for a
momma to let her children go away on their own.
Be careful out there in the great meadow, watch
out for things that scratch and claw, and come
right back home when the sun turns red in the
western sky."

Frog-child was so happy that he did three somersault hops, kissed his momma goodbye and headed off to go exploring. He jumped off his lily pad, swam across the pond, and hopped across the mud flats, past the swamp grass, and out into the great meadow.

On the other side of the great meadow, as the morning sun warmed the entrance to his rocky burrow, Snake-boy stretched out beside his mother. "Momma! I want to go exploring!" he said.

"Why don't you explore the boulders at the bottom of the hillside?" Momma-snake said.

"I went to the boulders yesterday."

"Then try the sand pit by the edge of the forest," suggested Momma-snake.

"Momma, I explored the sand pit the day before yesterday! I want to glide around the boulders, slide across the sand pit, and go out into the great meadow."

"The great meadow! Are you out of your mind?" shouted Momma-snake. "Why, there are things out there that will peck and bite and eat you up! Don't you even think about going out into the great meadow!"

"Oh, Momma," sighed Snake-boy, "I'm not a little baby anymore. It's time you let me grow up and go out exploring."

Momma-snake looked lovingly at Snake-boy.
"I suppose you're right, but it's hard for a
momma to let her children go away on their
own. Be careful out there in the great meadow,
watch out for things that peck and bite, and come
right back home when the sun turns red in the
western sky."

Snake-boy was so happy that he did three pretzel twists, kissed his momma goodbye and headed off to go exploring. He slithered down the rocks, around the boulders, across the sand dunes and out into the great meadow.

Snake-boy was moving carefully through the lush meadow grass. Suddenly he froze! Right in front of him was the strangest creature he had ever seen.

He quickly remembered his mother's advice and reared up in a tight coil. "Hold it right there!" he demanded in a nervous hiss. "You don't peck and bite, do you?"

The strange-looking creature thought carefully and answered in a trembling croak, "No, no, I don't peck or bite."

Snake-boy breathed a sigh of relief and began to uncoil.

"Not so fast!" blurted Frog-child. Snake-boy immediately recoiled in fright. "You don't happen to scratch or claw, do you?" asked Frog-child anxiously.

Snake-boy thought carefully and said, "No, no, I don't scratch or claw."

They both relaxed, looked at each other and, at the very same moment, asked, "HEY, WOULD YOU LIKE TO EXPLORE THE GREAT MEADOW WITH ME?"

They moved up face to face, gave each other a great big hug, spun around in a circle three times and said,

"You make a wish and I'll make a wish too,
And may your wish and my wish both come true!"

"What did you wish for?" asked Frog-child.

"I wished that we could play here all day long," answered Snake-boy. "What did you wish for?"

"Amazing!" exclaimed Frog-child. "I wished for the same thing! Let's go exploring!"

Off went the two new friends, searching into every nook and cranny that the great meadow could offer, and playing the most exciting games that they could invent.

When the sun was at its highest, they rested in the deep, cool shade and told stories of life on the lily pads of the pond and in the depths of the rock burrow. Snake-boy showed Frog-child how he could test the air with his darting tongue while searching for an earthworm snack. And Frog-child showed Snake-boy how he could use his flat tongue to snatch a fly right out of the air.

Then Snake-boy decided to teach Frog-child
how to slither! The little frog stretched his arms
and legs and wiggled on his belly through the
grasses.

"This is fun!" croaked Frog-child, "but it's a
little scratchy on my tummy. Say, how would you
like to learn how to hop?"

In no time at all, the little snake was coiled up
like a spring, bouncing all over the meadow.

"Wow!" hissed Snake-boy. "This is great, but it
sure is hard on my tail!"

The two friends slithered and hopped and
laughed until the sun began to glow red in the
western sky.

Frog-child looked up nervously. "My mother said to head right back home when the sun turned red."

Snake-boy looked thoughtfully at Frog-child. "My mother said the same thing. I have to go home, too."

They looked at each other for a moment and then blurted out, "WOULD YOU LIKE TO COME BACK HERE TOMORROW AND PLAY TOGETHER ALL DAY LONG?"

They moved up face to face, gave each other a great big hug, spun around in a circle three times and said,

"You make a wish and I'll make a wish too,
And may your wish and my wish both come true!"

"Ouch!" croaked Frog-child. "You're hugging me too hard!"

"Sorry," apologized Snake-boy, loosening his coils, "I didn't mean to hurt you."

"That's all right," said Frog-child. "Well, what did you wish for?"

"I wished that we could meet early in the morning and have the whole day to play."

"Wow, I wished for the same thing," smiled Frog-child. "See you tomorrow!" he shouted, as he moved away through the tall grass.

"Tomorrow," called back Snake-boy.

To anyone watching, that trip home must have seemed very strange. Frog-child quickly slithered all the way back home through the forest and the swamp grass, across the mud flats and right up to his lily pad in the pond. He smiled as he thought of Snake-boy bouncing into his burrow.

Meanwhile, on the other side of the meadow, Snake-boy was slowly making his way home. He hopped through the forest, across the sand pit and around the boulders. As he approached the rocky burrow, he laughed as he thought of Frog-child slithering into his lily pad home.

"Hi, Momma!" Frog-child croaked happily, as he slid up for a kiss. "What's for dinner? I'm starved!"

His mother took one look at Frog-child squirming around on the lily pad and screamed, "Land sakes, child! What in the world are you doing? You're going to scrape all the skin off your tummy!"

"I'm slithering, Momma. My friend, Snake-boy, taught me how to do it! We had so much fun playing in the meadow! What's for dinner?"

His mother turned a pale shade of green. "Did you say you were playing with a snake?"

"Yeah, Momma. We had a great time. What's for dinner?"

"Frog-child," his mother cried. "Come here and stop that ridiculous belly wiggling!"

The little frog hopped quickly onto her lap.

"Frog-child, snakes EAT frogs. He may have played with you all day, but snakes eat frogs: when he is hungry, he is going to eat you up!"

Frog-child was both horrified and bewildered. "But Momma, Snake-boy is my friend. We played together and told stories – and he taught me how to slither. He wouldn't eat me! He's my friend!"

"Frog-child," sighed his mother, "I don't want you playing with that snake again. Now eat your dinner."

But Frog-child could only think about his friend...

"Hi, Momma!" Snake-boy hissed as he hopped up for a kiss. "What's for dinner? I'm starved!"

His mother took one look at Snake-boy bouncing around on the floor and screamed, "Land sakes, boy! What in the world are you doing? You're going to break every bone in your body!"

"I'm hopping, Momma. My friend, Frog-child, taught me how to do it. We had so much fun playing in the meadow! What's for dinner?"

His mother nearly swallowed her tongue. "Did you say you were playing with a frog?"

"Yeah, Momma. We had a great time. What's for dinner?"

"Snake-boy," his mother cried. "Come here, and stop that ridiculous hopping."

The little snake slithered quickly onto her lap.

"Snake-boy, snakes EAT frogs. You may have played with him all day, but snakes eat frogs: when you get hungry, you eat him!"

Snake-boy was both horrified and bewildered.

"But Momma, Frog-child is my friend. We played together and told stories – and he taught me how to hop. I couldn't eat him!"

"Snake-boy," sighed his mother, "snakes eat frogs. Don't come home asking for dinner when you've been playing with a frog all day!"

Snake-boy slithered to the entrance of the burrow and thought about what his mother had told him.

The next morning, as the rising sun chased shadows across the hills, Snake-boy slipped out of his rocky burrow. Soon the great meadow stretched out before him in the morning mists. He glided silently into the damp grasses and waited for Frog-child.

The sun was high overhead before he moved
again. Frog-child had not come to the meadow.
Snake-boy decided to find his friend. Slowly and
carefully he made his way to the lily pads. Snake-
boy searched until he found a home exactly like
the one that Frog-child had described.

He coiled himself up onto his tail and peered through the reeds.

"Frog-child, are you there?" he hissed quietly. "It's me, Snake-boy!"

Frog-child peeked out from behind a lily. "Is it really you, Snake-boy? You came all this way just to see me?"

"You didn't come to the meadow this morning and I got worried," answered Snake-boy. "I wanted to see if you were still coming to play."

"I won't be able to play with you anymore, Snake-boy," said Frog-child softly. "Momma told me that snakes eat frogs. Is that true, Snake-boy?"

Snake-boy was silent for a long moment. "My Momma told me the same thing. I suppose it is true. Mothers are pretty smart. But I would never hurt you, Frog-child. I just want to be your friend."

"I just want to be your friend, too, Snake-boy. Exploring with you was the best time I ever had! We sure had fun."

"We sure did! Slithering and hopping around together – it was great! My Momma says I'm not to hop anymore. We can never play together again, Frog-child."

"Goodbye, Snake-boy. I'll sure miss you."

"I'll miss you, too, Frog-child. Goodbye."

And with that, the little snake slipped quietly away from the lily pads.

So it is to this day. When the sun floats hot and heavy in the afternoon sky, you can still see them sitting in the meadow. There is the snake, basking in the warmth of the sun, and there is the frog, crouching in the cool shade of the grass.

They never play together anymore, but they always watch each other from a distance and remember. If you listen carefully, you can hear them whisper, "What would have happened if they had just let us be friends?"

I wonder.

Ah, I see that you are thinking the very same thing that I am. So let me give you a big hug and we will spin in a circle three times. You make a wish and I'll make a wish, too, and may your wish and my wish both come true.